THIS WALKER BOOK BELONGS TO:

For Leroy

and his story

Also with love and thanks to my friends –

Tricia, Melanie,

Frank (especially for co-editing late at night in Cork),

Carolyn, Kate, Helen,

Paul and Sybille

and to Mark and Bonzo across the alleyway

Also to Cathryn

This story is based in and around
Salisbury Road and Beaumont Park,
Plymouth. Ordinary life.
Warmest thanks to Michael Hill
and to Helen Read at Walker Books.

First published 1997 by Walker Books Ltd
87 Vauxhall Walk, London SE11 5HJ

This edition published 1998

10 9 8 7 6 5 4 3 2 1

© 1997 Simon James

The right of Simon James to be identified as author
of this work has been asserted by him in accordance
with the Copyright, Design and Patents Act 1988.

Printed in Great Britain

British Library Cataloguing in Publication Data
A catalogue record for this book is
available from the British Library.

ISBN 0-7445-5491-8

LEON
AND
BOB

Simon James

WALKER BOOKS
AND SUBSIDIARIES
LONDON • BOSTON • SYDNEY

Leon had moved into town
with his mum.
His dad was away in the army.
Leon shared his room with
his new friend, Bob.

No one else could see Bob
but Leon knew he was there.
Leon always laid a place
for Bob at the table.
"More milk, Bob?" Leon said.

Sometimes Leon's mum
couldn't take Leon to school,
but Leon didn't mind.
He always walked to school with Bob.
He always had Bob to talk to.

Often, when Leon got home,
there was a letter waiting for him
from his dad.
Bob liked to hear Leon read it
over and over again.

One Saturday, Leon heard
some noises in the street below.
He saw a new family moving in
next door.
A boy looked up at Leon and waved.
Leon waved back.

That night Leon kept thinking
about the boy next door.
He decided to go round there
in the morning.
"But you'll have to come with
me, Bob," he said.

The next day Leon and Bob
ate their breakfast
very quickly.
Then Leon grabbed his ball
and rushed outside.

Leon ran up the steps
of next-door's house.
He was about halfway
when suddenly he realized
Bob wasn't there any more.

Leon sat down.
He was all alone.
He could ring the bell
or he could go home.
Why wasn't Bob there
to help him?

Leon rang the bell
and waited.
The door opened.
"Hello," said the boy.
"H-hello," said Leon.
"Would you like to go to the park?"

"OK," said the boy.

"I'm just going to the park, Mum,"
he called.

Together Leon and the boy walked
down the steps towards the street.

"My name's Leon," said Leon.

"What's yours?"

"Bob," said Bob.

MORE WALKER PAPERBACKS
For You to Enjoy

Also by Simon James

SALLY AND THE LIMPET

An unusual "green" tale about a girl who disturbs a
limpet and finds it's stuck to her finger.

"A gentle, thoughtful story with wonderful illustrations."
Practical Parenting

0-7445-2020-7 £4.99

MY FRIEND WHALE

The moving story of a boy and the whale with whom he plays each night.
Then one sad night the whale does not come…

"A lovely, gentle picture book with beautiful, blue illustrations."
Practical Parenting

0-7445-2349-4 £4.99

DEAR GREENPEACE

"One of the best books of the year, taking the form of letters between a
small girl and Greenpeace, to which she writes for advice about a whale
she finds in her garden pond… A perfect book for 3 to 5-year-olds."
Valerie Bierman, The Scotsman

0-7445-3060-1 £4.99

THE WILD WOODS

When Jess takes a walk in the woods with Grandad, she discovers some
natural wonders and learns a lesson too about wild things.

"A breath of fresh air… Witty and sparkling line-and-wash pictures…
Full of humour and vitality." *The Guardian*

0-7445-3661-8 £4.99